Fox Fire

ORCHARD
ReadAlouds

Jack Bobbin
Jill Bennett

Emily and Mr Prendergast
Shirley Isherwood

Rosie Rumpole
Annemie Heymans

The Tree House Trio
and the Pirates of Piccadilly
Effin Older

Poor Jack
Billy the Sailor
Una Power

The Giant Gutso
and the Wacky Gang
Paul Stewart

Class No. _____ J. _____ Acc No. C/55107

Author: GRANT G. Loc / NOV 1995

LEABHARLANN
CHONDAE AN CHABHAIN

_____

_____

_____

1. **This book m̶ ̶ ̶t three weeks. It is to be**
   ret̶ ̶ ̶ last date stamped below.
   ̶ ̶ arged for every week or
   ̶erdue.

Fox Fire

Gwen Grant

Illustrated by Toni Goffe

ORCHARD BOOKS

ORCHARD BOOKS
96 Leonard Street, London EC2A 4RH

ORCHARD BOOKS AUSTRALIA
14 Mars Road, Lane Cove, NSW 2066

ISBN 1 85213 337 6

First published in Great Britain 1991

TEXT © Gwen Grant 1991

ILLUSTRATIONS © Toni Goffe 1991

A CIP catalogue record for this book
is available from the British Library.

Printed in Great Britain

Chapter One

NOBODY KNEW HOW HEN COTTAGE
HAD MANAGED TO STAY UP FOR TWO HUNDRED
years. It was almost falling down. The tiles on the roof
dipped and sloped so sharply, they looked as if they
would roll off. The windows were as old as the roof
and rattled in the wind. Sam had pushed newspaper all
around the frame to keep the draught out. When
anyone closed the door, the windows shivered and
threatened to fall into the garden.

As for the front door, you couldn't use that at all.

Sam forgot about the door. He was always forgetting about it. One morning, he pulled it open and a

gust of wind caught it, slamming it back against the tiny room wall. The next second, the whole thing had come off in his hands.

"Oh, no!" he sighed. "Mum! Mum," he shouted. "The front door's come off."

His mother hurried through the little rooms to help him.

"Dear! More money." She hardly knew what to do. Since Sam's dad had died, there wasn't any money. They'd had to sell their house and come to live in Hen Cottage. It had taken every penny they had.

"Well, we'll just have to nail it on. We can't afford a new door, not just yet. Not till we get on our feet."

They looked through the empty doorway to the first thin whips of snow which swirled through the cold March air.

Mrs Rose shivered.

"We'll have to hurry up and do something, Sam. It's freezing."

Already, there was a line of snow on the carpet.

"I'll fix it," Sam said. "Let's just prop it up and then I'll fetch the hammer and nails."

Between them, they propped the door across the

opening. The wind blew the snow between the cracks.

Not for the first time, Sam wished his dad were there. He looked at the door and sighed. If his dad had been there ... he stopped. His dad wasn't there. He would have to do it himself.

His dad had taught him a lot of things but he hadn't taught him how to nail a door back on. Well, now he was going to learn.

He hurried to the shed. When he walked in, his face dropped. There were things everywhere. Piles of

cardboard boxes, old wooden tea chests, half-filled sacks and empty bags. Old drawers, broken chairs, plants, plant pots, spades, forks, hoes, brushes, a ladder and a pair of steps. They had all been moved into the shed when Sam and his mother had arrived at Hen Cottage and there they still were.

Sam rummaged through the boxes and bags. Nothing.

"I'll have to get this lot cleaned up," he muttered.

Whilst he was searching for the hammer and nails, he heard Roberta push open the gate. She always came the back way, along the garden and in through the hedge.

"Sam, Sam." He looked up as she tapped on the shed window. "What're you doing?"

She was cold. The snow was thick on her woolly hat.

"You'd better come in here," he called. "You look like a snowman."

Roberta pushed the door open.

"What're you doing?" she asked again and when he'd told her about the front door, she sat down on an upturned bucket and thought a minute.

"Perhaps Aunt Marion'll have an old door," she

suggested. Sam grinned.

"We've already got an old door. It's a new door we want." Then, "Ah! Found 'em." He turned to Roberta. "Do you want to come and help?"

The girl nodded.

When Sam and his mother had first come to the cottage, Sam had been homesick. He didn't know what to do in the country. All he knew was the town. There was no one near them to play with and he was lonely. Then Roberta had appeared.

She had stood at the garden gate and talked to him.

"Hello. Have you just moved here?"

Sam nodded.

"Yes." He had wanted to say more but didn't know how.

"I thought I hadn't seen you before."

There was a silence as Roberta looked at him.

"I've come to stay with my Aunt Marion. Well," she corrected herself. "She's really my great-aunt ... but she's very nice."

Another silence.

Then Sam made an effort. "Where are your parents?"

"They've gone to live abroad."

He was appalled.

"What, for ever?"

"Don't be silly. Just for a year. They've gone on a contract."

"Why didn't you go with them?" he asked.

Roberta shrugged.

"Children weren't allowed. So, here I am."

Sam thought a minute.

"Do you miss them?" He thought how much he missed his dad.

"Of course I miss them."

Sam had looked at the sky. It was late autumn then

and the sky was big and blue and gold.

"Do you want to come to Youth Club with me?" Roberta had asked.

He had kicked the bottom of the gate.

"I dunno." He wasn't sure about the Youth Club. "I won't know anyone there."

"But you'll get to know them if you come with me." Roberta paused, looking at him. "I'll come for you at six o'clock, shall I?" She turned to go, then looked back. "And don't be late, erm ..." She had smiled. "I don't know your name."

"Sam. Sam Rose."

"Don't be late, Sam." And she had gone.

Sam grinned now as he thought of that first meeting. Since then, he and Roberta had been good friends.

Now, they went together to the front of the cottage and started the long business of nailing on the door.

After several false runs, Sam threw the hammer down.

"This isn't going to work," he said. "I'll have to fetch some wood and nail that on to the door and then nail the whole thing on to the door frame."

Roberta blew through her gloves.

"It's freezing. Hurry up, Sam, we don't want to be here all day."

He went back to the shed to see if he could find some strips of wood. He thought he remembered seeing some amongst the junk. He was lucky. He found just the thing almost straight away.

When he got back, he said to Roberta, "You'll have to stand on the inside and hold the door." He looked at the whirling snow. "At least you'll be warmer there."

Sam hammered the strips of wood to the door and then, between them, they managed to haul the door into place. It fitted snugly into its frame.

As they worked, Roberta talked to him.

"Did you hear the fox last night?"

The boy nodded.

"Yeah. It was over the field. They're coming very close." He stopped hammering and thought about the hens who lived at the bottom of the garden. "I hope they don't take any more of our hens. We need them."

Roberta loved the foxes.

"But if they're hungry ..." she started.

"Even if they're hungry," Sam broke in at once,

"they can't have our hens. We're hungry, too."

Behind the door, Roberta scowled. The foxes took food where they could. She was mad about them. She often wished she were a fox.

"You don't know it was the fox who took your silly hens," she protested.

"They're not silly hens, they're just hens." Sam was sharp. "And of course it was the fox that took them." He wouldn't discuss it any more.

At last the door was nailed on. Sam stood back to look at it.

"It's not very good. It won't last long. One real push of wind and it'll fall down again."

His mother thought they'd done a good job.

"But we shall have to save for a new door now as well as all the other things." She pushed her hair back. "Never mind, we'll manage. Come on, I've baked some cakes."

But there was no time for cakes because Roberta suddenly remembered why she had come round in the first place.

"It's Aunt Marion," she started. "She wants to go shopping in the village and she wondered if you'd go with her."

Mrs Rose hurried to put her coat on.

"You should have said, Roberta. Imagine your poor old aunt sitting there all this time, waiting for me."

"I'm sorry. I forgot. What with the door and everything, it just went straight out of my head."

"I don't suppose there's any harm done." Sam's mother picked up her bag. "Come on, we'll go round together."

Chapter Two

WHEN THEY WENT INTO THE HOUSE,
THE FIRST THING SAM NOTICED WAS THAT, AS USUAL,
Mrs Spindle was wearing the red Russian tiara.
Today, the light caught the rubies and made it seem as
if the old lady was wearing a circle of fire on her head.

It made Sam's mother nervous to see the tiara.

"You should put that in the bank," she worried. "It's
so beautiful and it must be worth a lot of money."

Mrs Spindle laughed.

"It is valuable," she agreed. "But I like it here with
me. What's the use of a tiara if you never see it?" She
smiled. "There's two things I wouldn't be parted

from. My tiara and my lovely picture." She added casually, "I bought the picture when I was big game hunting in Africa."

Roberta looked at her aunt in astonishment.

"I never knew that," she exclaimed. "I never knew you'd been big game hunting."

"Oh, yes."

They all looked at the picture. It was a painting of a ship sailing full tilt along the top of the seas. It was all speed and ice and wind and sails. Sam thought it was brilliant.

Mrs Rose was curious. Well, she thought, if you believed Mrs Spindle, that explained the picture, but what about the tiara? Where had that come from?

"Ah, the tiara!" Mrs Spindle sighed. "My dear father left me the tiara. It came down through his side of the family so I do know some of its history."

"Do you know who owned it before your father?" Sam asked.

Mrs Spindle nodded.

"Yes, I do." She glanced at the clock. "If you like, I'll tell you what I know. We still have a little time. Or," she paused. "I could tell you something about big game hunting."

Roberta didn't want to hear anything about anyone killing the beautiful animals in Africa.

"I didn't kill them, my dear. I went hunting with a camera."

"Please," Sam put in. "Tell us about the tiara."

"Very well."

Sam's mother was anxious to be gone but when she saw her son's face, she sat down to listen.

"Through my great-grandfather, I have Russian blood in my veins," Mrs Spindle began dramatically.

"I never knew that," Roberta said. "I never knew you had Russian blood in your veins."

"Oh, yes."

"I shall have to work out a family tree." Roberta was thoughtful. "I might have Russian blood in my veins, too."

Sam wished his friend would be quiet. He was impatient to hear about the tiara.

"One of my ancestors was Catherine the Great," Mrs Spindle announced.

Mrs Rose stared into the fire. She wondered if the old lady just made up all these stories. If, really, there had never been any big game hunting in Africa and the tiara was nothing but gilt and glass.

"She wasn't always Catherine the Great." Mrs Spindle's voice softened. "She was just a peasant girl until Peter the Great married her in seventeen hundred and twelve. I understand he gave Catherine the tiara as a wedding gift."

Sam nearly fell off his chair. He quickly totted up. Why, that was nearly three hundred years ago. He looked at the tiara with new interest. Three hundred years ago it had started its life in Russia.

Mrs Spindle went on. "Peter was a great soldier but he got himself into a war with the Turks that he couldn't get out of. Catherine had to give up her jewels to save his life but she didn't give up the tiara. That stayed in the family."

"I never knew that," Roberta said again. "Is all this true? You've really got a Russian queen's tiara?"

"Empress, my dear. I have a Russian empress's tiara. When Peter the Great died, Catherine became Empress."

Great-Aunt Marion was enjoying herself.

"When my grandfather returned home to Russia at the beginning of this century, the tiara was given to him for safe keeping. There were rumours ... rumours of a revolution. He was entrusted with the tiara and it was arranged that, eventually, other members of his family would meet him at his home in London and reclaim the jewels." She shook her head sadly. "No one ever met him. We think they were all ..." she stopped and sighed. "All killed. Well, he put the tiara in a bank vault and gave instructions that no one must touch it for fifty years, just in case it was reclaimed." Again, she sighed. "Anyway, it lived in the bank all those years until I inherited it and brought it here with me. Beautiful things shouldn't be locked away. They should be used and loved. After all," she touched the tiara, "none of us, not even Catherine the Great, own things for ever. We're just the keepers of them."

Sam's head was full of pictures. Tiaras and empresses, soldiers and Turkish armies, revolutions and dry bank vaults.

Mrs Rose was sure it had all gone too far. Sheer romance, she thought. Filling the children's heads with nonsense. If that really was Catherine the Great's tiara, it would be worth a fortune and no one, not even Mrs Spindle, would have it in a cottage in the country.

She got to her feet.

"We'd better go now," she said. "Then we shall have time for a steady walk and we'll catch the butcher before he closes."

Mrs Spindle seemed to feel Mrs Rose's disapproval. She took off the tiara and put it carefully on the sideboard.

"You really ought to put that into the bank," Mrs Rose said again.

Sam looked at the tiara, glittering and shining. All those years it had glittered and shone. First in Russia and now, here.

The two friends went to the gate with Mrs Rose and Great-Aunt Marion. They watched them walk along the frosty pavement. When they reached the corner, Mrs Rose turned and waved. Sam and Roberta waved back.

"Do you think all that about the tiara was true?" Sam asked.

His friend shrugged. "I don't know. Could be, I suppose. That's the first time I've ever heard those stories."

The morning was almost over. It was very quiet on their own. The snow had stopped and a cold sun gleamed through the clouds.

"Listen." Roberta held a hand up. "Can you hear them?"

Sam nodded. He thought the whole world must be able to hear them. It was so clear. The sharp triple bark of the dog fox echoing over the frozen fields. Then, the answer. The spooky high scream of the vixen.

He shivered.

"That scream gives me goose pimples," he said.

Another sound filled the air. The sound of the hens in the hen coop. They were squawking and clucking as if their lives were being threatened.

"The foxes!"

Sam turned from the gate and ran down the path. Those foxes! They got bolder and bolder. Now, they came right into the garden, in the daylight. He pushed the gate in the hedge open and hurtled across the grass. Round the apple tree, over the hard brown earth and then he saw it. The tawny red gave it away. A fox stood looking at him. The bright eyes glinted. The sharp face grinned.

"Go away," Sam shouted. "Just get out of here."

The hens were flapping and running up and down the coop, in and out of the henhouse.

"Oh, stop it, you stupid hens," Sam roared. "He can't get in at you."

By the time Roberta reached him, the fox had gone.

"I never saw it. Why did you shout at him? You're really mean, Sam. You know how much I've wanted to see him. It was the big one, wasn't it? I just know it was. It was the biggest and the best of them all, wasn't it?"

"Yes. And if he comes here again to steal the hens, I'll ... I'll ..." Sam didn't know what he would do.

He walked round and round the hen coop, testing the wire here and pushing against the wooden posts there. It was quite secure. He had stretched wire over the top of the coop as well. The first two weeks they had lived in Hen Cottage had seen four of their hens gone.

"We can't afford it," his mother said. "We have to keep the foxes out."

Now, Sam stood and looked over the cold fields.

Foxes, he thought. Foxes!

Chapter Three

ROBERTA WAS FURIOUSLY ANGRY
WITH SAM. SHE TURNED ON HER HEEL AND MARCHED
up the garden path.

"You knew I wanted to see him," she repeated.

"See him in your own garden," Sam retorted. "I
can't let him come near the hens. We can't afford to
lose any more. He wants to keep away from me, that
fox does, because if he doesn't ..."

"You wouldn't dare do anything to him," Roberta
broke in.

"Oh, wouldn't I? You just wait and see. If he takes
one more hen, I shall do something."

They argued and argued. In the end, Roberta crossly pushed back through the hedge gate. There was a mist falling over the fields and the gardens. Through it, the tall dead stems of flowers, iced with frost, looked like herons standing in water.

"Well, I think you're mean, Sam."

Roberta walked away from him, then jumped with surprise. At the side of the house, standing almost hidden in the mist and shadow, was a young man.

"Oh!" Roberta put her hand to her mouth. "You made me jump."

She waited until Sam had caught up with her and was standing by her side.

"Hello," Sam said. "Can we help you?"

The young man smiled and stepped forward.

"Am I glad to see you!" he began. "I thought no one was in. I've been knocking on that door for ages. I've come from the Social people. They've sent me to tidy up the garden." He stared at them. "Didn't tell me nothing about no kids though. They said it was an old woman, living on her own." He glanced down at the papers in his hand. "This is eighty-four, isn't it? Eighty-four the Road?"

Roberta nodded.

"Yes." Then she told him how she had only just come to live with Great-Aunt Marion and how Sam didn't live there at all. "He lives next door," she finished.

"Right." He grinned at them, then walked to where they were standing. He peered through the mist. "It certainly looks in a bit of a mess."

It was now so cold, Sam thought the earth would crack in two.

"Let's get on, shall we?" the young man said. "Can you show me where the gear is?" He smiled at their puzzled faces. "The spades ... and all that."

"Oh! They're in the shed," Roberta told him.

"And where's the shed?" He was laughing now. They were all laughing.

Sam stepped forward.

"I'll show you where it is." He looked at the garden. "But you won't be able to do any digging. The earth is frozen solid."

"Oh, you let me worry about that. Spring's just around the corner. It's all starting to warm up."

The children looked at the frozen world.

"It is," he insisted. "It's starting to warm up. We can't see it but it's there all right. Down in the earth, the warmth's there. Besides, I'm a good gardener, I am." He paused. "And, anyway," he went on, "when them at the office say 'dig', I dig."

Soon, he had the big spade in his hands. He was called Frederick, he told them. After his dad.

Frederick worked for some time. The soil was heavy. Cut with frost, it was heavy to dig and heavy to lift. The two children worked alongside, sweeping up the dead leaves, stuffing them into bags ready to take away. They were joined by a robin, who hopped up and down the newly turned earth. There were lean pickings. Nothing seemed to be moving in the close-packed soil.

27

When the wind got up again, the mist started to clear.

"This is hard work," Sam grumbled but Frederick carried on with his digging.

Sam stared at the garden. Yes, it looked much better.

At last, Frederick stood straight. He listened. It was a day for listening. Every sound carried on the clear air. The bells in the churchyard rang twelve times.

"Dinner time," he said.

"I'll go and make you a cup of tea," Roberta offered but Frederick said no, she needn't bother, he had a flask of tea with him.

The young man pulled a pile of sacking out of the shed and sat down on that. He poured out the steaming tea and threw crumbs to the robin.

Roberta's cheeks were scarlet with cold. She rubbed her hands together.

"I'm going inside," she said. "I'm frozen. Are you coming, Sam?"

The boy shook his head.

"No. I think I'd better get off home, make sure everything's all right."

Just as he turned to walk back to Hen Cottage, there

was a tremendous crash.

"What was that?" Roberta stood still, listening.

They all waited. Waited for another bang but nothing else happened. There was no more noise and then, with a sinking heart, Sam realised what the sound must have been.

"Oh, no," he groaned. "It's the front door, isn't it? It's gone and fallen off again. It's this wind."

He kicked at a stone.

"I'm really fed up with that door. It just won't stay on." Miserably, he pushed the gate open. "I shall have to do it all over."

Frederick looked across at him.

"What's the matter?" he asked. "What's all this about a door?"

When Sam told him, the young man screwed the cap back on to his flask and put away his sandwiches.

"Come on. I'll help you put it on properly. When we're finished, it won't fall off again."

They worked at the door all through Frederick's lunchtime and then Great-Aunt Marion and Mrs Rose were back.

They had piles of bags. Piles of shopping.

"Whose is the old van?" Mrs Spindle cried, once

she was in the house. "It's blocking our gate."

Roberta told her about Frederick and about the garden and about Sam's front door.

"Of course he's got to have a cup of tea." The old lady was firm about this. "You fetch him in here and I'll put the kettle on."

She dumped her bread and meat, fruit and jams, her paper bags and packages on the table, on the chairs and on the sideboard. Frederick didn't want to go into the house.

"I always like stopping outside," he said. "I've only got to get near cups and saucers and something breaks." But at last Roberta persuaded him.

He didn't stay long.

"I'll do another couple of hours," he said. "And then I'll finish until the morning." He looked at the sky. "Looks like more snow. You can't work in the snow."

They all went with Frederick into the garden. He didn't get any more work done at all. Great-Aunt Marion walked up and down, up and down, showing him this which must be done and that which had to be seen to.

Before he could do anything, it was time for him to go.

Just before Frederick went, Sam heard the old familiar sounds of the hens.

"That fox," he shouted. "He's back. Come on, Roberta."

Sam went helter-skelter up the garden, through the hedge gate and down to the hen coop. Great-Aunt Marion followed slowly. The hens were screeching as if they had already lost their heads.

"Look. Look." Sam pointed to the ground. "They've been." He knelt to the pawprints on the thin snow. "Here's the big one. And there's the little one." He squatted on the ground, scowling out into the field. "I'll catch you one day," he promised. "I'll frighten you out of your wits."

Mrs Spindle rapped on the top of the henhouse.

"Do be quiet, hens," she ordered. "Such fussy creatures." Then, she turned. "Now, where's Rober ... oh, there you are. Why, Frederick must have gone home. I quite thought he was with us, too." She shook her head. 'Well, well."

The old lady made her careful way back up the garden.

Sam stared over the fence, into the clump of trees at the end of the little field before the wide green and brown sweeps of land began.

He became aware of Roberta now, standing at his shoulder. She stepped across to the gate which led into the paddock and climbed the top bar.

"He's there, Sam," she screamed. "I can see him. Oh, you lovely thing. You lovely, lovely thing."

There were three short barks.

"I can see them," Roberta shouted again. "Two of them. They're running like crazy. Oh, they're so ... so ..." and then she lost her footing and tumbled head over heels into the thick grass below.

"Ouch!" The fall winded her. Sam had to climb

over and help her up.

"I should have left you." He was grumpy.

The trouble with Roberta, he thought, was that she just did not understand.

Chapter Four

SAM DIDN'T GO BACK INTO THE HOUSE WITH ROBERTA. HE LEFT HER IN THE GARDEN, waiting for another glimpse of the fox. They had quarrelled quite fiercely.

"You're so bad-tempered," she had said. "Those lovely foxes. How would you like to be out in the cold and the snow with nothing to eat?"

"I wouldn't go stealing other people's hens, that's for sure," Sam had returned.

"They're not stealing your hens. You haven't seen them." Roberta was white-faced with anger. "You've no proof."

Sam had turned on his heel and gone home. Now, he looked out of the window to see if he could see his friend. The garden was empty. He could see right down to the bottom, down to the hen coops. It was all quiet.

Roberta had waited and waited to see if the foxes would return. When they didn't, she had gone slowly up the garden and back into the house. She couldn't stop thinking about them. What did they get to eat? She knew they were thin. Even their rough coats hadn't been able to hide that. She woke up at night sometimes, worrying.

Her aunt was in the kitchen, making tea.

She stopped what she was doing when she saw Roberta and looked past the girl out of the back door.

"They'll be all right, you know."

"Who will?"

"Who will?" Great-Aunt Marion smiled. "The foxes, that's who. They'll get enough to eat. They scavenge."

"They do not." Roberta couldn't bear to hear her aunt saying that those beautiful animals scavenged, as if they were ... they were ... she gave up. She liked all animals who had to search out their food. She respected them. She just liked and respected animals, full stop.

"Of course they scavenge. They knock over dustbins and scoff what they can get out of them. They steal hens." Her aunt looked up. "Oh, yes, they do. As you already know. As a matter of fact, they pinch any food that's not nailed down—and that as well if they can get it free."

Roberta said nothing at all. They sat in silence, drinking the hot tea. The girl couldn't settle. She wondered if the vixen would have babies in the spring. She thought of last spring, when she and her mum and dad were holidaying at Great-Aunt Marion's, how she had caught a glimpse of the vixen and her cubs. How the vixen had sensed she was there and how she had stood and pointed with her muzzle and her cubs had hurried to her side, almost as if she had called them, one by one, as Roberta's mother sometimes used to do.

Roberta wondered how that was done. How could the vixen have called her babies without making any sound?

They were so clever, she thought. So clever and so beautiful. And so hungry, a voice in her head added.

She stared out of the window. She couldn't see Sam's hen coops from the kitchen. She realised she was alone in the small snug room. Great-Aunt Marion had gone upstairs. Roberta fastened her coat. The foxes might come back, she thought. They just might.

When her aunt called down, there was no answer. Roberta had gone.

Sam hadn't been at home all that long when the fuss started. He heard the sound of a voice shouting. At first, he couldn't make out what it was. He went back to the window. No, it wasn't Roberta. Then, as the voice grew clearer, he realised it was Great-Aunt Marion.

"Mrs Rose! Mrs Rose! Oh dear, oh dear, Mrs Rose, where are you? Are you there?"

Sam's mother lifted startled eyes.

"Whatever's going on?"she exclaimed. "That sounds like Mrs Spindle."

She rushed to the front door and flung it open and once again, the door came off in her hand and fell flat on the ground.

"Oh, Sam," Mrs Rose breathed. "I'm sorry," and then Great-Aunt Marion was on top of them.

"Help. Help. Robbery."

The moment she saw Mrs Rose, the old lady started to cry.

"But whatever's the matter?"

"My tiara! It's gone! My beautiful tiara. Gone! Stolen! I've had to send for the police. I've told them they must come at once."

"Oh, you shouldn't have sent for the police yet." Sam's mother was concerned. "We ought to have had a good look for it first."

"But I've looked. I've looked everywhere." Great-Aunt Marion's face was streaked with tears.

"No one could have stolen it." Sam was sure of this.

"No one has been in your house. Roberta and I were here all the time you and Mum were in the village."

"Frederick." Mrs Spindle said the name with a flat heaviness. "It was him. He stole it. He was in the house. I gave him a cup of tea to keep out the cold and this is how he repays me. He steals my tiara. I knew I should have asked where he came from. Heartless, they are, all these young people. Heartless."

"But ..." Sam tried to break in.

"I gave him a cup of tea, out of the goodness of my heart, and he steals my tiara. Well." She wiped her eyes. "The police will catch him and make him give it back."

"But ..." Sam tried again. No matter how hard he tried, he couldn't get a word in.

They listened to the old lady for some time. She grew more and more upset.

"You must calm down," Sam's mother said, worried about her. "You must try and stop crying, Mrs Spindle." She turned to Sam. "Where's Roberta? She should be here with her aunt."

The boy shrugged.

"I don't know where she is. I left her down the garden. That's where she was the last time I saw her."

39

Mrs Rose put an arm around the old lady's shoulders.

"Sam, go down and see if Roberta's there. We need her here."

He shook his head.

"She wasn't there, Mum. She'd gone. When I looked out of the window, she'd gone."

"Sam." His mother's voice was firm. "Go and see. She might be out of sight somewhere."

At that moment, Roberta came through the hedge gate. She looked pale and cold.

"But where have you been?" Mrs Rose was impatient. "Never mind, never mind, don't tell me. We must get your aunt into the house. Try and calm her down, Roberta. This sobbing can't be good for her."

Sam told Roberta what had happened. All the time he was speaking, Mrs Rose was ushering the old lady to her own cottage.

"I was out in the paddock," Roberta said bleakly. "I didn't know anything about all this. I wish you hadn't let her send for the police."

Mrs Rose broke in.

"We didn't let her do anything, my dear. It was

done before she came round. Now, come and help me settle her down."

They all trailed into Mrs Spindle's cottage.

"You certainly took your time coming," Sam grumbled but Roberta didn't answer.

Once in the house, Mrs Rose bustled around, making tea and building up the fire.

"Hot sweet tea," she said to Great-Aunt Marion. "That's what you need. Get some colour back into your face." She glanced at Roberta. "And you've been outside too long. You're frozen. Goodness," she went on. "I shall have you both ill at this rate."

The girl tried to smile but her lips seemed too chilled to move.

"I'm fine, honestly. I'm just a bit cold."

Mrs Rose gave her the tea.

"Here, drink this. No," she said. "Please don't argue, Roberta. Drink it. It'll do you good."

Great-Aunt Marion wept softly.

"And to think," she moaned. "I gave him a cup of tea and this is how he repays me."

"But the tiara was still there after Frederick had drunk his tea," Roberta put in. Sam was relieved

someone was getting in a defence for Frederick. "If I saw it after Frederick had had his tea, then he couldn't have taken it."

"He didn't even want to come into the house," Sam said. "Did he? Don't you remember? He said he didn't like getting near cups and saucers because they always got broken when he was around."

"He would say that, wouldn't he?" Mrs Spindle sniffed. "Especially when he was planning to rob a poor defenceless old woman."

Sam thought of the big game hunting. He decided once for all that the story couldn't be true. Not unless

Mrs Spindle had been a different person then. He looked at her. She suddenly seemed tiny and ancient. He felt sorry for her, and sorry for Frederick, too. He wished the tiara was safe and sound on the old lady's head.

"But it was on the sideboard after Frederick left, Aunt Marion." Roberta tried again.

There was a short silence and then Mrs Spindle returned to the attack.

"But he didn't go with us to the hens, did he? It was then he must have stolen into the house and … and taken his chance. Oh dear, oh dear."

"There, there." Mrs Rose comforted her. "Look, why don't we have a good search for it, before the police come. You would look silly if we found it down the back of a chair."

Great-Aunt Marion stared at her.

"I certainly would," she said sharply. "Especially as there is no chair big enough for it to fall down the back of."

"It couldn't have been Frederick, Mum." Sam was unhappy. "He was so kind to us. He spent all his lunch hour helping me with our door. He helped me nail it on again."

"Yes." His mother sighed. "Oh well, I suppose we'd better see if we can find the wretched thing."

They couldn't find it. They searched high and low but the tiara had vanished.

"I said you should put it in the bank." Mrs Rose was hot and worried. "Now what shall we do?"

And then the police turned up and they had to hear the whole story all over again. They had to have a full description of the tiara and of Frederick and his van.

Sam thought he had never felt so miserable. Poor old Frederick, he worried. What was going to happen to him?

Chapter Five

THE POLICE WERE PATIENT WITH
GREAT-AUNT MARION. THEY SAT DOWN WITH HER
and took out their notebooks and listened carefully as
the old lady went through the whole story again.

Sam felt he couldn't stand to hear it once more. He
was sure Frederick had nothing to do with the missing
tiara. He said as much to the policemen.

"He was never in the house on his own," he told
them. "And he wouldn't have stolen it. He didn't even
want to come into the place."

His mother said, "You'd better go home, Sam.
Wait for me there. I won't be long."

45

Roberta was silent and unhappy. Sam wandered out of the cottage and down the path. He didn't feel like going home. He walked to the gate and stood looking down the road. He wished he could see Frederick. See Frederick and what? he thought.

"Sam, wait for me." Roberta's voice was strained. She hurried down the path towards him. "Isn't this awful?" she said.

Sam was quiet. He didn't feel like talking. He didn't feel like doing anything very much, except standing at the gate and looking down the road.

"We ought to warn him," he said suddenly. "One of us ought to find him and warn him."

"Yes."

Sam wondered where Frederick was. He looked down the lane again. The world was turning whiter and whiter, colder and colder. All the puddles were shiny with ice. The grass and the leaves on the hedges were doubled in size with their thick frosty coating. He thought you could almost hear the frost floating out of nowhere and settling on the trees and the branches. He wondered if he and Roberta stood still long enough if they, too, would gather frost and look twice as big.

"He hasn't stolen the tiara," he repeated. "I'm sure he hasn't."

Roberta was unfriendly. "How do you know?" she demanded. "You blamed the foxes for taking the hens and I just bet they didn't do that either."

"Oh, Roberta, this is something quite different."

"No, it isn't. If you don't believe Frederick stole the tiara then why do you believe the foxes stole your hens? You didn't see them do it, did you?"

The boy shook his head.

"No, but this is different, Roberta. Really it is."

"All that makes a difference," the girl said crossly, "is that Frederick has two legs and my foxes have four."

Sam lost his temper.

"They're not your foxes. Foxes don't belong to anyone. You shouldn't want them to, either."

"Don't be so silly, Sam. Of course I don't want them to belong to anyone, but nobody else looks out for them. You don't. But I do and I'm telling you, my foxes didn't steal your silly hens."

"Well, I don't care if they did or didn't," Sam shouted untruthfully. "All I care about is Frederick."

Roberta frowned and turned away. She marched

back into Great-Aunt Marion's cottage and Sam was left standing on his own.

"Well," he muttered, "I might as well go and look for him."

He unlatched the gate and stepped out into the lane. He wandered down the road towards the woods. In the hedge side an old beer can glittered.

He wondered idly if he would recognise Frederick's van when he saw it. He'd only seen it briefly. As he turned into Winter Lane, he did see it. He stopped, shocked at actually seeing the van, and then he thought he might be able to do something after all. He might be able to warn Frederick.

He hurried down the road. The van was standing dark and empty.

The boy peered in through the windows. No one there. He went to the edge of the woods which flanked the road.

"Frederick," he shouted. "Where are you?"

The young man stepped out from between the trees.

"Who wants to know?" he said.

"Oh!" Sam was taken aback. He hadn't really expected Frederick to be there. He must have been

standing behind a tree, he thought. Hiding. Why?
Why was he hiding?

"What are you doing?" he asked, suspicious.

"I was . . ." Frederick brought his hands from round
his back. Sam could see he had a rabbit dangling from
each hand.

"You've been poaching."

Frederick's face was set and serious.

"So what?"

Sam looked at the rabbits. He could see the blood
which darkened their muzzles speckling their fur. He

was reminded of the tiara. The frozen drops of blood were like red jewels. He shivered. Then he realised he couldn't see a gun.

"You haven't been shooting them, you've been setting traps," he said with horror. "Those rabbits could have been trapped for hours. Don't you know what they do to themselves when they can't get free? They try and chew off their own legs. How could you, Frederick? How could you do that?"

He turned from the young gardener and stormed away. He wouldn't tell him, he wouldn't warn him, he deserved all he got. Setting traps. It was the cruellest thing you could do to any animal.

"Sam." Frederick called him. "Sam." The boy turned. "Sam, I'm sorry."

"You'll be even more sorry when they get you," Sam shouted. He was blazing with anger.

"When they get me," Frederick repeated. "When who gets me? What are you talking about?"

"When the police get you. They're coming after you, you know."

Frederick didn't laugh. "What, for poaching?"

"For stealing."

"A rabbit or two? Don't be so daft."

"Not for stealing a rabbit. For stealing a tiara."

"A tiara!" Frederick stared at him. "I've never even seen a tiara. I wouldn't know a tiara if one stood up and bit me."

"You stole Mrs Spindle's tiara." Sam was having trouble speaking. He could see the rabbits. He couldn't tear his eyes from them.

He had a sudden picture of the foxes dead, like the rabbits. He shuddered. No. No, he didn't want the foxes to have the hens but he didn't want them dead like that, either. He would just have to make sure they couldn't get into the hen coop. Especially the big dog fox.

"I never stole no tiara," Frederick repeated, indignant.

"I know you didn't," Sam said. But now, he didn't know that at all. Not when Frederick was poaching. Not when he was already taking something that didn't belong to him.

"Anyway," he went on lamely. "The police are at the cottage. They were asking for a description."

"That's stupid. They've only got to ring the Social to find out where I live."

Sam shrugged. "I suppose they'll do that, as well."

Frederick walked to the back of the van and flung open the doors. Sam hardly dared look. Had he got more dead rabbits in there? He had. Sam turned away.

"I thought I'd tell you." He regretted warning Frederick. "I'm sorry I did now. Anybody who traps animals deserves to be locked up."

"Look." Frederick held out his hands. "I'm sorry. They earn me a bit on the side, that's all. You can't live without money."

"You shouldn't trap them."

"How should I do it? Run after them?"

Another silence and then the quiet air came alive with noise. They both heard it. The shriek of a siren.

"It's them." Sam was thunderstruck. "It's the police. They're coming after you."

"They aren't coming after me. What, for a blinking tiara or something?" The young man tried to take things steadily. He caught up the dead rabbits from the back of the van and slung them into the darkening woods. "There," he said. "Now I haven't got anything in here at all. They can't prove a thing."

He slammed the doors shut and walked to the front of the vehicle.

"I'll give you a lift home," he threw over his

shoulder. "It's getting dark. You shouldn't be down on this road when it's dark."

Sam shook his head.

"No, thanks. I'll walk across the fields."

"Suit yourself."

Frederick stopped by the side of the van and looked back up the road. His face was strained.

"Can you see them?" he asked. "Is that their blue light?"

Sam felt a little sorry for him. He turned. At first he could see nothing at all, but then he saw the blue beam, flickering in and out of the trees, as if a giant needle and thread were stitching up the landscape.

"Yes," he confirmed. "That's them all right." He turned back to Frederick. "But they won't ..."

He had no chance to say more because the next second Frederick was in the van and the engine was roaring into life. The van pulled violently away. Then it stopped as suddenly as it had started.

Frederick leant through the window. "Blinking tiara," he said. "What a cheek. Well, they're not getting me. I've done nothing wrong."

"Then you should tell them. You shouldn't run away."

"I'm not running away. I've done nothing to run away for, but I'm not hanging around for them." Frederick was angry and scared. "I'm going home. You can please yourself what you do."

He gunned the engine and was gone.

Chapter Six

SAM STARED AFTER THE VAN. HE WISHED FREDERICK HAD WAITED UNTIL THE POLICE had arrived. He was sure it would have been the best thing to do.

He could hear that the van was not taking the bends in the road. It was going much too fast. He could smell burning rubber. Frederick must be taking an inch off his tyres every time he cornered.

He looked behind him. The blue light was coming closer and closer. What a racket, he thought, and then he had to make a fast jump into the hedge.

There was no room in the narrow roadway for cars

to sweep out from the grass verge. As the police car hurtled past, Sam felt a sudden rush of air from its speed.

"Gosh!" he said aloud. "They nearly got me then."

He stood in the new dark of the road, listening. The white of the frost lightened the outside of the woods but inside, where the trees hugged each other close, Sam knew it would be as dark as ever.

He looked over the hedge across the fields. There was still light enough for him to walk by.

He stiffened. What was happening? He was puzzled. Instead of going further away, the sounds were coming closer. At once he understood what Frederick had done. He had taken the van off the road and into the fields. That was why the engine noise was so loud.

Quickly, Sam climbed the fence, gingerly pushing aside the stray limbs of hawthorn which tugged at his jumper and jeans. He dropped on to the hard iron earth of the field and started to run. If he was quick, he might see Frederick. This field and the two beyond would lead him back to his own house, so if he didn't see the van, he wouldn't have lost anything.

It was hard going, running. He had to be careful not

to slip and twist an ankle because the earth didn't give
to his feet.

There! There was the van, careering across the top
field.

"Oh, Frederick," the boy shouted. "You dope.
You should have waited."

And there! There was the police car, centimetres
from the van's back bumper.

Sam hoped Frederick didn't suddenly slam the

brakes on. If he did, there would be one great crash.

He ran on. Overhead, he saw the flickering lights of a light aeroplane coming in to land at the little airport nearby. He stopped to watch it. It looked very close. He felt if he lifted a hand, he would be able to touch its wings.

For a moment, the roar of the aeroplane drowned out the sounds of the van and the car. Then, Sam was at the top of the field and the plane had vanished behind a clump of trees.

Sam made for the big gate. He nerved himself to touch the iron fastening. It was so cold, he was frightened it would stick to his skin. It didn't and with relief, he pushed the gate open and slipped through, shutting it fast behind him.

It was at that moment he heard the harsh noise of crashing metal.

Someone's misjudged, Sam thought. He shook his head. Poor old Frederick.

The boy hurried along the side of the big field. The field was very long. Once, he tripped and banged his head. It was like hitting stone. He lay winded on the earth. Almost in his ear, he heard the sharp barks of the foxes.

He lay still and looked up at the wide sky. It was full of melting fluid stars. Sam forgot Frederick and the police car. At his side, a fox appeared, trotting briskly along the path. Its eyes glittered redly. The fox was so close that for a second, Sam felt surrounded by eyes. Then, the animal was gone, deep into the safety of the hedgerow.

The boy sat up and rubbed his head. That bang had shaken him. All those eyes! He shivered as he thought of the fox and where it could be going.

He felt a sudden blinding certainty.

"That fox is going to our house." He was absolutely sure of it. "He's going after our hens. Well, you're not getting them," he shouted now. "They're our hens. You wait, you fox, you. Just you wait. I'm coming. I'll teach you to steal hens."

His head was forgotten. Sam leapt to his feet and set off running. This time, he veered away from the site of the crashed cars. The hens were more important. Let Frederick sort things out for himself.

He went through another gate and down the side of the home field. He was coming closer and closer to the house. He sensed the fox was in front of him. He had the strongest feeling of being a fox himself. He grunted impatiently. Faster, faster. He took another tumble and heard the barking of the foxes again.

He was almost there. In the far field, he could see the spread of lights. The blue light of the police car swept round and round.

Then, he saw him. Sam stood still. The big dog fox was motionless. He was almost leaning on the fence which separated the small paddock from the end of their garden. It was as if he was thinking. For a second, the fox was there and then, for all his size, he had

moved like an arrow, slipping through the space at the bottom of the fence and vanishing into the garden.

Sam jerked forward.

"Rah rah rah," he yelled. "Rah rah, get out of here, you fox, you."

He was close enough now to catch a glimpse of the thin clever face, the crafty sparkling eyes, then it was gone. As fast as he could, Sam clambered over the fence. Where was that fox? Where had he gone? He was furious. Just let it touch one feather, one feather, that was all.

For a minute or two, back in the field, he'd wanted to run with the fox instead of against him but now the animal was actually in the garden, sniffing around the hen coop, he felt all the old rage coming back.

"Get get get," he bellowed. "Get get get."

"Why don't you just shut up?" The voice, lazy and cold, drifted out of the darkness.

"Who's that?"

"Who do you think?."

He knew who it was. Roberta.

"What are you doing here?"

Roberta stepped forward. "Admiring the view. What else?"

"Oh, very funny."

The girl pointed. "I was watching the lights. That's a police car, isn't it?"

Sam ignored the question.

"Have you seen a fox?" he asked.

"A fox?"

Sam leapt off the gate.

"Yes, a fox. The fox. The big fox. The one that just came in here. I saw him come in, Roberta, so don't lie. You must have seen him come through the fence."

"You've got foxes on the brain. There's no fox here."

Sam felt something was wrong. But what? No fox would make friends with a human being, not when they were full grown. And yet ... yet ... he looked at Roberta.

"There was a fox," he insisted. "And he came through here. I saw him."

The girl shrugged.

"So? There's no fox now."

Sam pushed past. He didn't believe her. He shouted again, half expecting the fox to dart out, to make a dash for the fence, but nothing happened. Nothing moved.

"Are you coming back to the house?" Roberta asked.

The boy shook his head.

"You've been up to something," he accused. "I know you, Roberta. I know what you're like about those foxes. I'm warning you. If he comes and takes another hen, I'm going to get a gun."

She laughed.

"You and Robin Hood." She moved away from him and set off up the path.

"I shall kill them if I see them," he shouted after her. "I shall tell the farmer ..." His voice trailed away. He hadn't meant to say that.

Roberta stopped and stood, motionless, in the middle of the path.

She turned.

"If you ever did that," she said, "I would never speak to you again."

Sam swallowed hard.

"Then don't you encourage those foxes down here."

She was gone, walking towards the cottage as if he were invisible. Sam heard a soft rustle of paper. He frowned. That Roberta. What was she up to? She was up to something, he was certain of it.

"What are you up to now?" he yelled, but Roberta just laughed and started singing.

Her voice floated through the crisp dark air.

"Foxy would a–hunting go,
Hey–ho, said Foxy.
Foxy would a–hunting go
Whether Sam Stuffy would let him or no,
Hey–ho, said Reynard the Foxy."

The boy stamped his anger on the path. One of these days, he thought.

Before he went in, he checked the hen coop. It seemed as safe as houses. Sam scowled. Even a house wasn't safe where there was a fox. He could hear the soft clucking of the hens. They were settling down for the long winter night.

He banged around a bit more but no fox broke cover. In the end, he left the henhouse and the garden to itself and went in.

Once in the warm little room, he told his mother about the fox.

"He's out there somewhere," he said. "I searched and I searched but I couldn't find him."

He thought of the fox lying hidden, those bright fierce eyes sparkling like fire. He thought of the pointed nose and the long mouth. He could almost see the animal laughing at him. See the white teeth grinning.

Sam jumped to his feet.

"Where are you going?" his mother asked.

"I'm getting the torch and I'm going to have another look."

"I'll come with you."

They took the torch and went back down the garden but there was nothing, only the long blue light of the police car and the shiny twin moons of Frederick's headlamps.

Apart from that, there was nothing else at all.

Chapter Seven

IT WAS DARK WHEN SAM WOKE UP. HE LAY QUIET, LISTENING. SOMETHING HAD WOKEN him. Then, he heard it. The sound of rain on the window. He thought of the foxes, out in the wind and rain.

"That should keep them at home," he muttered and turning over, he snuggled deep into the bed.

Even through the duvet which was bunched over his head, he heard the sound again. It sounded more like hail than rain. Then it came once more and now Sam noticed there was a silence after each little bout of noise.

Curious, he got out of bed and went to the window. The moon was shining and he could see a white and frozen world.

A white world, he thought. What about the rain? Shouldn't that have cleared away the snow?

As he pressed his forehead against the window pane, the sudden sharp tiny blows on the outside of the glass made him pull away in astonishment.

"What's going on?" he muttered. He opened the window and pushed it wide.

"Sam. Sam, can you hear me?"

The whisper carried clearly. Sam pulled himself on the window sill and looked down.

"Who's there?"

"You always say that," a furious voice replied. "Who do you think's here?"

"Roberta. Is that you?"

"No," his friend said crossly. "It's King Kong and Superman. Of course it's me. Who else would it be?"

Sam almost wished it had been King Kong and Superman. They couldn't be any more scratchy than Roberta, he thought.

"Well, what do you want?"

"I want you to come down."

"To come down? What for? It's cold out there."

He peered at the dark figure below him. "Shouldn't you be in bed, Roberta?"

"Sam, come down. I've got Frederick with me."

Sam's mouth dropped open.

Without another word, he pulled the window shut and put his slippers on. At the last minute, he dragged an old jumper over his pyjamas.

Going through the cottage in the dark was eerie. Sam had to go slowly and carefully down the old

wooden stairs. It was as if they were alive, the way they groaned and creaked and complained. At every step, he expected to hear his mother's voice calling him but he made it to the back door without any problems.

Opening the door was difficult. The big black iron key grated in the lock. He was hot with the effort of keeping everything quiet. When he finally got the door open, Roberta and Frederick were bundled up in the shelter of the porch.

"You took your time," Roberta grumbled. "Come on, then, let us in."

Sam stepped back and opened the door wider.

"You'll have to be quiet," he whispered. "My mum's not a very good sleeper."

"She doesn't have to be," Roberta said shortly. "Because I'm not stopping to talk. I just want you to hide Frederick until the morning."

Sam looked at the young man.

"But what are you doing here, Frederick? I thought the police had caught up with you on the field."

Frederick looked tired.

"No." He shook his head. "I escaped and ran across the field into your garden. I hid in your henhouse."

"In my henhouse!" Sam felt really fed up. His hens. Again. "Blow it, Frederick, first the foxes and now you. We'll get no eggs at all at this rate. They don't like being scared, you know. It puts them off laying. Why did you go in my henhouse?"

"You know why. They think I've pinched that tiara and I haven't. I ain't never seen a tiara. Not never."

They were all frozen, standing with the door open. The snow had started falling again and was blowing in.

"We'll freeze to death out here," Sam whispered.

"I've got to go." Roberta was anxious. "I've left the door unlocked. Sam, can you keep Frederick until morning and we can think what to do?"

The boy nodded slowly.

"I suppose so."

Hardly were the words out of his mouth than Roberta had turned away and was hurrying back home.

"You'd better come right in," Sam said.

When he and Frederick were both inside and the door was locked, he poked the last red cinders of the fire into new life and stacked it with logs. As the wood burned and the room grew warm, Frederick told him what had happened.

"I just thought they wouldn't believe me," he started. "So, when we was tearing across that there field, I opened the door of the van and jumped out."

"Was that when it crashed?"

The young man nodded. "Yes. I wedged the accelerator with a stick. I knew it wouldn't go far on that ground, it was like a frozen sea. Bump bump bump, we went. But when I got it going nicely, I jumped out and rolled into the hedge." He grinned. "They never saw me." He started to shiver. "I don't suppose you've got anything to eat, have you?" he asked.

Sam was worried.

"But what are you going to do now?"

Frederick shook his head.

"I dunno." Sam could see he was very tired. "I s'pose I shall have to keep moving. I've only made it ten times worse for myself. Now, they'll be sure I stole that thing."

Sam nodded. He could see how that would be.

"You'll just have to go to the police station and explain. I'll come with you."

Sam went into the pantry and fetched out a loaf of bread. He handed the toasting fork to Frederick and between them they toasted a pile of thick brown slices. The boy spread deep layers of butter and jam on the toast.

"Sam." The voice drifted down the stairs and made them both jump. "Sam, is that you?"

"It's my mum," Sam whispered, then called out, "it's all right, Mum. It's only me. I was hungry. I'm making some toast."

"Well, don't be long, and, Sam ... make sure you leave the fire safe."

Frederick ate the toast as if he hadn't eaten for weeks. Sam crept upstairs and fetched a couple of blankets and a pillow. The young man put them on the sofa and stretched out.

"I can't remember ever being so tired," he said and instantly fell asleep.

Sam went quietly to bed. He set the little alarm clock. He must wake up before his mother. If she went down first and found Frederick, there would be trouble.

Frederick would have to leave the house first thing in the morning. He would have to go and hide somewhere, but not in his hen coop, Sam thought darkly. Somewhere else. That would give him and Roberta time to work out what to do next.

But in the morning, when he got up, his mother was downstairs before him.

"And just who," she said, staring at Frederick, "is that?"

Sam sighed.

It looked like being a very difficult day.

Chapter Eight

IT WAS SOME TIME BEFORE THINGS
WERE SORTED OUT. MRS ROSE INSISTED THAT
Frederick go straight home.

"I'll come with you, if you like. Then you can tell
your mother and father exactly what you've told
me." For Frederick and Sam had told her the whole
story.

"They won't believe me," Frederick protested.

"Well, they certainly won't believe you if you
don't go and tell them. They must be worried to
death."

Mrs Rose went to get her coat. She was angry with

74

Sam, letting Frederick spend the whole night in the house. "My goodness," she thought. "It was quieter when we lived in town."

Frederick had a painful interview with his parents. His dad kept saying, "I don't believe it."

"I'm afraid it's all true," Mrs Rose put in.

"Where is this tiara now, then?" his father asked.

Sam shook his head.

"That's the trouble. We don't know."

"I don't think it was very fair of that old lady to accuse our Frederick of stealing it, especially when you say it was seen after he'd been in the house. Seems to me," he paused, "seems to me this mess is all her fault. She's the one to blame."

Mrs Rose stood up.

"We must go," she said. "Mrs Spindle is an old lady. I'm sure the police will sort everything out."

Sam wished he felt as sure, but he didn't. The tiara was missing and no one knew where it was.

They all left the house together, for Frederick's dad had rung the police station and now he was taking his son to see the officer in charge of the whole business.

"Can I come as well?" Sam asked, but his mother wouldn't hear of it.

"I think between you, you've been in enough trouble."

"That lad of mine is seventeen years old," Frederick's father said. "And he hasn't got the sense he was born with. Poaching! I just hope I don't hear of that again." He looked at Sam. "And you're as bad," he said sternly. "Mixing everything up."

Sam flushed.

"I thought I was helping. I'm sorry."

Frederick held out his hand.

"You've been a good pal to me. Thanks, Sam."

They shook hands. Mrs Rose turned away.

"Good luck, Frederick," she said and walked on. Sam followed.

As they walked, Sam hoped aloud that Frederick wouldn't get into too much trouble.

"Not much chance of that hope coming true," his mother said. "And that brings me to you."

Sam didn't enjoy the walk home. His mother seemed to think everything was his fault and she told him so, over and over again.

"I don't know how you could have been so foolish," she finished.

By the time they reached Hen Cottage, Sam was wishing he had never seen Frederick, Roberta or anyone else in the whole world.

"Best of it is," Roberta said when she came to call for him, "they don't seem to believe me when I tell them the tiara was in the house after Frederick had gone."

Sam was feeling sore and angry after the telling-off his mother had given him.

"How is it," he attacked, "that I always get into trouble for the things you do?"

Roberta stared at him.

"What do you mean?" she said. "What have I ever done that's got you into trouble?"

"What have you ever done that's got me into

trouble?" Sam repeated bitterly. "Oh, nothing. Just a little matter of bringing Frederick to our house in the middle of the night and making me let him stop till the morning, that's all." The more Sam thought about it, the angrier he got. "Why didn't you take him into your house? You've as much room as we have."

"Don't be silly, Sam. I didn't make you do anything. And, anyway, how could I have taken him into Aunt Marion's? If she'd seen him there, she'd have shouted the place down. She never would have believed I'd let him in, would she? By the time Aunt Marion had finished, Frederick would have been locked up for a million years."

"Yeah, well ... you've always got a reason for everything, you have," Sam said crossly.

"That's because I am reasonable. If I had gone to warn Frederick, I would have made a better job of it. It was you who panicked him. You caused the whole thing to happen."

Sam thought he would burst with rage.

"Now, look here, Roberta. You just stop saying those things and mind your own business."

"Ha!" Roberta tossed her head. "You want to take your own advice. If Frederick hadn't been driving as if he were on a race track, the police wouldn't have bothered with him at all." She glared at Sam. "You've done with Frederick what you did with the foxes. Given a dog a bad name. You were sure, really, that Frederick had taken the tiara, weren't you?"

"No, I wasn't," Sam retorted with indignation. "I didn't think it was him at all. I never did. Not ever. Not from the beginning."

"Then why warn him? You were just the same with the foxes."

"Will you stop that," Sam protested. "I know it was the fox who took the hens because I saw him do it. It wasn't the same thing at all with Frederick. It was you blaming him, not me." He paused. "Are you quite sure you didn't see the fox when you were out there last night, before you dragged Frederick to our house?"

Roberta smiled, but her smile was unfriendly.

"I would have told you if I'd seen him."

Sam knew he was the very last person she would have told if she had seen one fox, two foxes or three hundred. He thought Roberta was good at seeing just what she wanted to see. She had seen the tiara but she hadn't seen the fox.

"It doesn't seem fair," the girl swept on. "Everybody thinks Frederick took it. They'll always think so too, unless ..."

"Unless what?"

"Nothing." Roberta turned her back on him and strode away.

Sam watched her go. He sighed. He wished Mrs Spindle had never owned a red tiara. He thought of Frederick at the police station and hoped he was getting on all right. He wandered back home and started to prepare the mash for the hens' dinner.

When it had cooked and was hot and steaming, he hauled the big bucket down the garden.

In the sunlight, he could see quite clearly where the fox had tried to get into the hen coop.

"You!" he shouted at the empty fields. "I'll get you, you see if I don't."

That made him feel a lot better but then, having put down the mash bucket so that he could open the hen coop, he got a bad shock. By the side of the henhouse, he could see the clear white of a splintered bone.

Sam felt sickness rising in him. What was that? He wanted to walk away and leave it alone but knew that he couldn't. He had to know what it was. Carefully, he moved across and kicked the bone with his foot. It rolled into the open and he saw that it was heavy with red meat.

He frowned. The foxes must be spreading their net wider, he thought, for this was no hen. This was part of another animal.

He looked out at the countryside. It was bare and cold. There was snow on the fields and he knew how hard the ground was. The foxes must be getting desperately hungry.

He drew in a deep breath. He knew he would have to tell the farmer. If the foxes were taking sheep or the first early lambs, they would have to be stopped.

Sam stared at the bone again. "Hang on," he muttered. There was something about it that made him kneel to examine it more closely. Yes, now he could see that it was a clean cut. He stood and stared thoughtfully down the garden. Things were starting to add up.

He left the bone where it was. He would see to that later. Right now, the hens were clamouring for their food. He picked up the mash bucket and, unlocking the door of the hen coop, stepped in to the wire enclosure.

He liked giving the hens their mash. He liked the fuss they made and the racing about. He was so absorbed in what he was doing and in watching the hens and listening to them, that he forgot the world outside the hen coop.

He smelt the fox before he saw him. The raw wild smell with its strong musky overtones tickled his nose. Without thinking, he stood still and silent. When he turned his head, he did so with extreme care.

There he was, just outside the wire, tugging at the bone. Sam felt a wild flame of excitement. It was the big dog fox. The one who killed the hens. There was a gleam of sunshine and the fox lifted his head to the light. In the sudden strong burst of sunshine, Sam saw the same red eyes he had seen the night before.

He blinked, then shook his head. There were a hundred eyes glittering at him. He closed his own eyes, then opened them slowly. Now he could see what was wrong.

The fox was wearing a collar of eyes.

He had the tiara around his neck! So that was where it had got to!

Instinctively, Sam stepped forward. The fox looked up at the movement. For a moment or two, they stared at each other. The boy could see the fox's eyes weren't red at all. They were more yellowy, amber, gold, and they sparkled.

Sam scowled. That fox looked just as if he was laughing. If I catch him, he thought, he'll laugh on the other side of his face. But before he could move, the fox was trotting down the side of the garden.

Sam flung himself out of the henhouse. He caught a glimpse of the animal shoving under the bottom of the fence but then something went wrong and it got caught. Held fast.

As the boy went closer, he saw that a bramble had snagged on the tiara.

The fox turned, snarling, its eyes full of pain and terror.

"It's okay," Sam soothed. "I won't hurt you."

He winced as he watched the fox trying to get its head free, pulling so violently the collar bit into its neck. The animal yelped with pain.

"Just stand still," Sam pleaded, "and I'll help you."

The fox barked and barked until, with one last giant effort, it had twisted its whole body under the fence, dragging its head clear of the tiara. As it came free, he staggered, straightened, turned, then loped swiftly across the paddock, disappearing into the trees.

"And that's that," Sam said. "Don't come back any more." Then, forgetting the fox, he turned his attention to the tiara.

Chapter Nine

THE TIARA LAY ON THE GROUND. THE
BOY WALKED OVER AND PICKED IT UP. IT WAS HEAVY
in his hand. He touched the sparkling red stones,
feeling their smooth coldness. He held the jewelled
circlet to the sun and watched as darts of fire filled the
garden.

"You can come out now," he said aloud, admiring
the way the shafts of red light stained the snow.

The evergreens moved and Roberta stepped in
front of him.

"Clever," she said. "How did you know I was
there?"

85

"Because I could see you from where I was standing." He pointed to the henhouse. "You can see a lot from there and, anyway, I expected you, Roberta. You knew about the bone, didn't you?"

She nodded.

"Yes." His friend took the tiara out of his hand. "I was in the house yesterday when the fox came in, but he didn't see me. They're all starving, Sam. He must have smelt the meat. He jumped up and knocked it off the sideboard but the tiara was on top of the meat and it fell over his head." She stopped. "I tried to catch him but … but he was so scared. He ran off. He didn't even take the meat with him."

"So you decided to bring it down to him?" Sam interrupted. He was angry.

"Yes, I decided to bring it down to him."

"And the tiara was round his neck?"

"Yes."

"And he ran off with the tiara?" His words were short and clipped.

Now, Roberta glanced at him, as if she was aware of his anger for the first time.

"Yes, he ran off with the tiara and I couldn't tell anybody. If I had, they'd have hunted him."

Again, he broke in.

"So, instead of hunting the fox, they hunted Frederick."

She was defiant.

"Frederick can speak. A fox can't. They would have shot him. He wouldn't have stood a chance."

"Frederick didn't stand much chance either." Sam thought of their friend at the police station. "He could be in a lot of trouble, you know, and it's all your fault."

Roberta tried to look sorry but Sam knew her. He knew she wasn't sorry at all.

"Surely you understand," the girl went on. "I couldn't run the risk of someone shooting him. I just couldn't and that's all there is to it."

"And what about Frederick? He's at the police station right now."

"No, I'm not."

Both the children whirled round. Frederick was leaning against the apple tree, looking at them.

"I did whistle," he said. "But you were that busy rowing." He stopped, then went on. "I heard what you were saying." He looked at Roberta. "Didn't you think about me at all?"

Roberta had paled but she met Frederick's eyes firmly.

"Frederick, I'm sorry but I had to think about the foxes. I was going to tell the police. I wouldn't have let you get into any really bad trouble." Her voice trailed away.

"I don't know what you call bad trouble then." Frederick's voice was almost cheerful. "I think I've already been in bad trouble. You and them foxes. You're mad about them, aren't you? It's okay, Sam," he went on. "The police believe me. They believe I didn't take the tiara. That's why I'm here. I figure somebody owes me an apology and I've come to collect it."

"Well, I'm sorry," Roberta said instantly.

"And I'm sorry," Sam added.

"Then there's just one person left." Frederick turned and walked back up the garden. Sam looked at the footprints in the snow. Frederick was a neat walker. There was one line of footprints down and one line going back. Roberta must have walked down the outside of the garden, the fresh meat in her hand.

"Frederick's going to your aunt's," Sam said.

"Yes. I'll go in a minute. I just need you to hear the story, that's all. The only way I could think of to get the fox back into the garden was to bring the meat down here." Roberta carried on as if they hadn't stopped talking.

Roberta noticed all the paw-prints in the garden. They weren't clear like Frederick's. He knew why. They'd been made in the first fall of snow and then more snow had fallen lightly on top of them, filling in the stark black marks.

"Those foxes must have had a picnic in here last night," he said. He looked at Roberta. "You're crackers, you are, do you know that? Crackers. I could have been here with a gun when they came into the garden." He held up his hand to stop Roberta speaking. "If I'd had a gun, I would have shot them."

Roberta stared at Sam as if she had never seen him before. All at once, it seemed as if their friendship was in danger.

"You're a townie," she said. "You don't know anything about the country."

"I don't have to. All I have to know is that the foxes were killing my hens. You want me to understand about them, Roberta but can't you understand about my hens?"

The girl didn't reply. She started to walk back up the garden, placing each foot neatly inside the prints made by Frederick.

"That's what you were doing last night, isn't it?" Sam pursued. "When I heard that paper rustling. It was you wrapping up the meat again. You had to take it back into the house then because you knew I'd see it."

"I'm going in. I don't want Frederick to upset Aunt Marion."

Sam followed her. He felt very sad and almost scared by the coldness that had come between them. Step. Step. Step. Roberta was slow.

"You're supposed to care about the foxes." He had to go on. He had to make her see. "You could have got them killed. When are you going to stop encouraging them to come close to the houses? If you don't stop soon, there'll be no foxes left. The farmer will find out where they come and when they come, he will, you know he will, especially when the lambs are in the fields." Sam wished the lambs were in the fields now and that it was warm and sunny and green, and that he and Roberta were friends once more. "If the farmer knows where they come then, he'll kill them."

They were up at Hen Cottage. Without a word, Roberta went through the gate and closed it behind her.

Sam leant on it, staring over. He could see Frederick standing by the back door of Mrs Spindle's cottage.

As he watched, the door opened and Mrs Spindle was framed in the doorway. She gave a cry of alarm when she saw the young man.

"Oh dear, it's you again. What have you come to steal this time?"

Before Frederick could reply, Roberta had broken in. "He didn't steal your tiara, Aunt Marion." She held the tiara out to her aunt. "It's here."

The old woman was so surprised that for a

moment, she said nothing. Then, she took the tiara
and looked from Roberta to Frederick.

"What happened to it?" she asked.

"It fell over a fox's head when he came in to steal
the meat," Roberta explained tersely.

"I see." Mrs Spindle lifted a corner of her apron and
rubbed at the tiara. The red jewels became radiant with
light as she polished the dust and grime off the stones.

Sam thought he had never seen anything quite so
beautiful and yet, once he tore his eyes away, he could
see that Frederick was upset and again, he wished he

had never set eyes on the tiara.

"That's twice you've accused me of stealing," Frederick said. "You got me into a lot of trouble, you did."

"Then I'm sorry." Mrs Spindle was direct. "I am very sorry indeed, Frederick."

"You should think before you speak," Frederick ploughed on. "You're old enough to know better. When you tell stories, you should think about what they mean and about what they can do."

Mrs Spindle nodded.

"Yes." She was thoughtful. "You're quite right." She looked at the tiara and then at Frederick. "Would you care to hear about when I went big game hunting in Africa?"

"No," Frederick said. "I wouldn't."

"Ah! Well then, perhaps you'd care for a cup of tea instead?"

"No," Frederick said again. "I wouldn't. I hate tea and now I hate stories, too."

This upset Mrs Spindle.

"I am so sorry. Really, truly, sorry."

The young man turned away and, noticing Sam standing at the gate, waved. "G'bye, Sam. I'll see you some time."

He walked to the side of the house, turned the corner and was gone.

The old lady lifted the tiara and put it on her head. "What I might do," she said, "is leave the tiara to you, Roberta, when I die." Roberta couldn't have cared less. "And then, you could sell it and use the money for the foxes."

Great-Aunt Marion smiled sadly but Roberta didn't smile back. She walked to the corner of the house and watched Frederick as he went through the garden gate.

"Goodbye, Frederick." She lifted her hand and waved. "Goodbye."

Sam left and and headed towards his own house. A strong wind was getting up, so before he went in, he checked the front door. As he reached the door, a violent gust of wind pulled it out of its frame like a felled tree.

BANG!

The door hit the ground with a solid clap of sound. The next second, Sam heard Roberta shout, "Is that your door again, Sam?"

"Yeah."

The girl appeared at his side.

"I'll help you fix it, if you like."

Sam nodded.

"If you want."

Roberta glanced up at the sky.

"It's all finished with now, Sam. Done. Like Frederick said, spring's coming and soon it'll be warm. There'll be plenty of food when it's warm."

Sam hoped Roberta was right. He hoped that spring really was coming and that the foxes would leave the hens alone and that he and Roberta could keep on being friends.

He stared into Great-Aunt Marion's garden and wondered why he hadn't noticed there were tiny buds on the trees.

"I don't suppose we'll ever see Frederick again," he said at last.

And there was the front door too, he thought. That needed proper fixing.

Roberta shook her head.

"No," she agreed. "Frederick won't ever come back here."

And, in her heart, for the very first time, she hoped the foxes wouldn't come back either.